12/8
Withdrawn
www.hants.gov.uk/library
Hampshire
County Council
Love
YOUR LIBRARY
Tel: 0300 555 1387

D1355465

C016527918

A Home Full of Friends

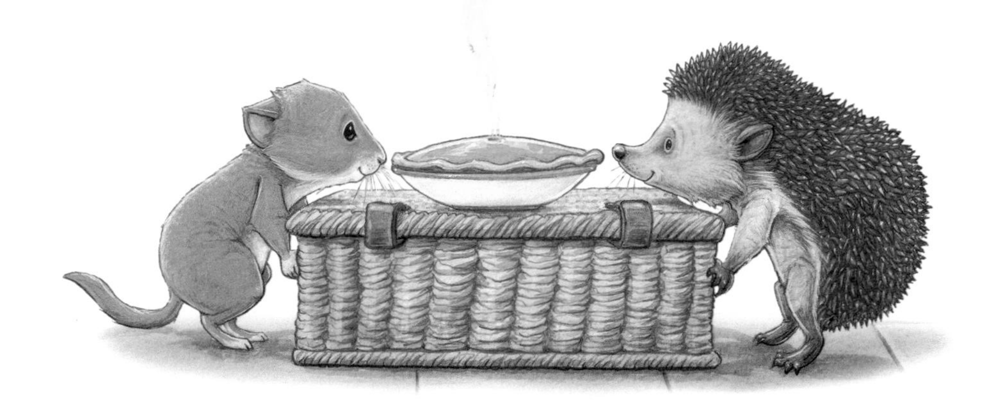

First published in Great Britain in 2017 by Hodder and Stoughton

This edition published in 2017

www.badger.org.uk

A CIP catalogue record of this book
is available from the British Library.

ISBN: 978 1 444 92057 4

10 9 8 7 6 5 4 3 2 1

Printed and bound in China.

Hodder Children's Books
An imprint of
Hachette Children's Group
Part of Hodder and Stoughton
Carmelite House
50 Victoria Embankment
London EC4Y 0DZ

An Hachette UK Company
www.hachette.co.uk

www.hachettechildrens.co.uk

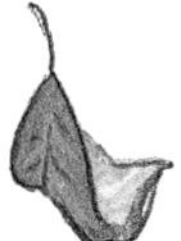

A Home Full of Friends

Written by Peter Bently
Illustrated by Charles Fuge

Bramble was looking for nuts by the river
when a sudden fierce storm made him shudder and shiver.
"Oh bother! I'm bound to catch a cold in this storm!
I'm heading back home where it's cosy and warm!"

Then – CRASH! Bramble nearly jumped out of his skin.
"Whatever was that? Is the sky falling in?"

The wind had blown over a rotten old tree.
"My house!" Snuffle squeaked. "It's as flat as can be!
Now there's nowhere to keep out the wind and the wet.
Unless, little Bramble, there's room in your sett?"

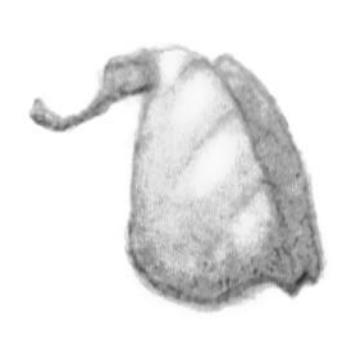

"Oh dear," fretted Bramble. "My sett is a mess,
and I haven't much space or much dinner but... yes."
"Thanks!" said the dormouse. "See you tonight."
And she scampered off into the grass, out of sight.

Then Bramble met Tipper the Toad by a flood.
"My house!" Tipper grumbled. "It's full up with mud!
Is there space in your sett, little Bramble, to stay?"
Bramble looked worried but answered, "OK."

Bramble walked on through the icy cold breeze
and bumped into Boo running round in the trees.

"My nest has been buried by leaves!" babbled Boo.
"Any chance, little Bramble, of staying with you?"
"It'll be a tight squeeze," Bramble said. "But all right."
"Thanks!" said the hedgehog. "See you tonight."

“Oh dear!” Bramble sighed when he got through his door.
“Do I have enough food in my kitchen for four?
And where will they sleep? I really can’t say.
Oh, I shouldn’t have said they could all come and stay!”

But Bramble was kind. He would never say no
to three little creatures with nowhere to go.

He searched every drawer,
every cupboard and shelf.

There was just enough food
for three guests and himself.

Then he looked in his junk room and found some old plates,
an old wooden stool and a couple of crates.

But still Bramble worried. “I’ve only one bed!
We’ll all have to squash in together,” he said.
“The toad’s bound to snore. The hedgehog’s all prickly.
And the dormouse’s whiskers are sure to be tickly!”

He was worrying still when he heard a loud knock.
He opened the door – and got a big shock...

There on the doorstep were Snuffle and Boo,
and Tipper with all of their families too!

“Oh dear!” Bramble groaned. “I hate to sound rude.
You’re welcome to stay, but I haven’t much food,
and there’s only one bed. It’s just not enough!”
“Don’t worry,” grinned Snuffle. “We’ve brought loads of stuff.”

To Bramble's amazement,
in marched his guests
with things that they'd managed
to save from their nests.
"My goodness!" smiled Bramble.
"There's so much to eat!
And blackberry pie –
that's my favourite treat!"

They had a fine feast round the cosy warm flames.
Then Bramble said cheerfully, “Let’s play some games!”

First they played pin-the-tail.
That was good fun.

Leapfrog was next.
The toads always won.

Last, they played skittles out in the hall.
The hedgehogs took turns
to roll up in a ball.

"And now," Bramble smiled. "It's bedtime, I think.
How about a story, and a tasty warm drink?"

They all gathered round in a big snuggly heap
to hear Bramble's tale before going to sleep.

With the embers still burning all toasty and bright,
Bramble tucked everyone up for the night.

"My home's a bit crowded, it's true," Bramble said,
as he took off his slippers and climbed into bed.

"But I really don't mind if it feels a bit small...

...for a home full of friends
is the best home of all."

To Eunice - C.F.

For Connie and Sissy - P.B.